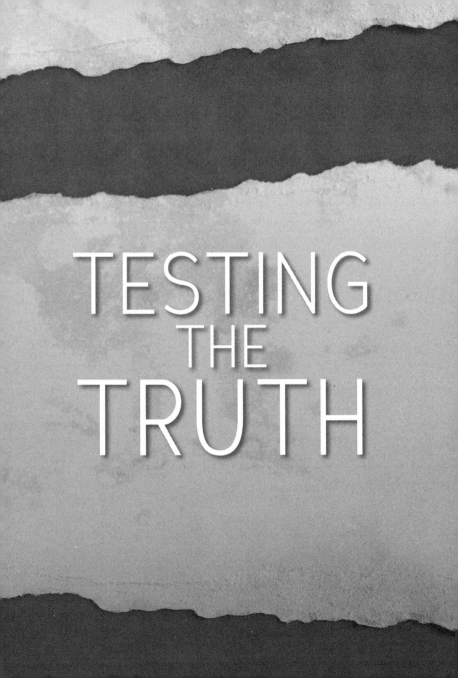

TESTING
THE
TRUTH

SUSPENDED

TESTING THE TRUTH

Shannon Knudsen

darbycreek
MINNEAPOLIS

Darby Creek
A division of Lerner Publishing Group, Inc.
241 First Avenue North
Minneapolis, MN 55401 USA

For reading levels and more information, look up this title at
www.lernerbooks.com.

Front Cover: © iStockphoto.com/jarenwicklund (teen guy); Cover and interior:
© iStockphoto.com/Sorapop (ripped paper).

Main body text set in Janson Text LT Std 12/17.5.
Typeface provided by Adobe Systems.

Library of Congress Cataloging-in-Publication Data

Knudsen, Shannon, 1971– author.
        Testing the truth / Shannon Knudsen.
            pages cm — (Suspended)
        ISBN 978-1-4677-5708-9 (lbg. : alk. paper)
        ISBN 978-1-4677-8095-7 (pbk. : alk. paper)
        ISBN 978-1-4677-8828-1 (eb pdf)
        1. Cheating (Education)—Juvenile fiction. 2. Photography—Juvenile fiction. 3. High school teachers—Juvenile fiction. 4. Truthfulness and falsehood—Juvenile fiction. 5. Decision making—Moral and ethical aspects—Juvenile fiction. 6. High schools—Juvenile fiction. [1. Cheating—Fiction. 2. Examinations—Fiction. 3. Teachers—Fiction. 4. High schools—Fiction. 5. Schools—Fiction.] I. Title.
PZ7.K78355Te 2015
[Fic]—dc23   2014040368

Manufactured in the United States of America
1 – SB – 7/15/15

CHAPTER ONE

Ever notice how the principal's office is the ugliest part of the whole school? It's like a shrine to administrative power. You've got the row of file cabinets, the uncomfortable guest chairs, the unreadable diplomas hanging on the walls. The lights that make everybody look like they haven't slept for two weeks. The window with a parking-lot view. And don't forget the monster desk with the fake wood surface, straight from Office Max.

I'd had plenty of time to study my surroundings while Principal Juarez listened to himself talk. He was gravely disappointed with my behavior. What had I been thinking, falsely accusing a member of his staff in such a public way?

I liked that "his," as if I'd intended to personally insult Juarez himself.

"It's not a false accusation," I said for about the twelfth time.

"That's not what Ms. Opal says." His face was red from the temper tantrum he'd just thrown. "She's been a respected teacher at this school for eight years. And everyone knows that photos can be altered—*and* that you're an expert at photography."

"Right. Photography," I said. "Not digital manipulation. You do get that those are two totally different things?"

"Watch your tone, Kai Tamura," Juarez said. "You're in a lot of trouble here." He flexed his knuckles, which were beefy like the rest of him, and stared me down.

I took a deep breath and reminded myself that Juarez had nothing on me. Nothing. The only evidence—the photos—backed up my story one hundred percent.

"All I wanted to do was tell the truth about Ms. Opal," I said.

"No, you wanted to humiliate her, destroy her career, and turn the entire community against her," Juarez said. "If you'd just wanted to tell the truth, you could have brought those photos straight to me instead of posting them online."

He kind of had a point there.

"I didn't want it to get swept under the rug," I said. Probably not the best response, given the way Juarez's expression hardened.

"Mr. Tamura, you've never gotten into any serious trouble at this school. But your conduct in this matter is too serious to take lightly. As of today, you are suspended for the next week."

Suspended?

I tried to process what I'd heard. A suspension would go on my permanent record. I was about to start applying to colleges, and every single one of them would see this black mark against me. Not only that, but my parents would probably disown me. A son of theirs, shamed before the entire school?

No. This was not good.

"Principal Juarez," I began. "I don't think this is fair, considering—"

"It wasn't fair of you to treat Ms. Opal the way you did. But you've made your choices, and now you'll face the consequences. You have parking privileges, is that correct? Your car is here today?"

I nodded.

"Well then, get your things and go home. I'll see you a week from today at one o'clock in this office. Ms. Opal will be here as well, and you'd better be prepared with a sincere, detailed apology for what you've put her through."

I tried again to protest, but Juarez cut me off.

"This is the part where you say 'Yes, sir'

and get out of my office. I'll be phoning your parents this evening to inform them of your suspension. You might want to prepare them."

I muttered something that sounded like "yissr" and got out of there, still stunned. I hadn't done anything wrong. Well, actually, I had. That just wasn't what I'd been suspended for.

CHAPTER TWO

Two days before my chat with the principal, I was somewhere I wasn't supposed to be, doing something I wasn't supposed to do. The place was a teacher's classroom way after the final bell had rung. The something was stealing a test. Or trying to steal one, anyway. I wasn't having much luck finding it.

Let me say right here that I'm not a cheater, generally speaking. I know it's wrong and all that. But I was pulling a C in Ms. Opal's trig class. If I ended up with a final grade like that, my parents would nail me to my desk chair for the entire spring. And I had a girlfriend, a driver's license, and plenty of plans for my senior year that did not involve being grounded.

I'd studied my butt off, but I needed a boost. A big one. So I made an exception to my usual policy of honesty. I did feel bad about it. I truly did. Not only because it was wrong but because Ms. Opal happened to be my favorite teacher. She was one of the ones who got to know us as individuals. Like, she knew that I loved photography and hated French, and she knew about my friend Vince's amazing singing voice. She was a nice person, in other words. So I wasn't proud of what I was trying to do.

It takes some planning to steal a test. I started my research a few weeks ahead of time, just in case I decided I needed to go forward with the theft. My first idea was to hack Ms. Opal's laptop, but like I told Principal Juarez, I'm into photography, not computers. Then I noticed that she kept papers locked in her desk at the back of the classroom. The night before a major exam, those papers would surely include the answer key, right?

After that, it was simple. I watched some lock-picking videos online. It's pretty amazing what you can do with a couple of paper clips if you know how. I practiced on my dad's desk at home until I could open it in less than three minutes. I figured I'd pick Ms. Opal's lock after school, photograph the answer key, and put it back. She might notice the drawer wasn't locked the next day, but I was betting she'd just unlock it without checking first. Even if she did notice, the worst thing that could happen was that she'd delay the test and change it. She'd never know I was the one who picked the lock.

So there I was, the day before the test, putting my plan into action. I sneaked into Ms. Opal's classroom twenty minutes after the final bell. By then, she'd be gone for the day. I knew the janitor would be around eventually, but I'd studied his rounds. He always started in the cafeteria, so I had a good two hours before he got to this part of the school.

The lock turned out to have a different make than the one on my dad's desk, but I kept my cool. A couple minutes later, it finally clicked open. Jackpot! Inside the drawer, I found a batch of homework papers, the standardized tests we'd taken that day, some memos from the principal, and a utility bill. But no test and definitely no answer key. All my planning was for nothing.

And that's when the classroom door opened.

You know those moments where you have to act in a heartbeat, have to make a choice so fast that you can't think first? And sometimes you end up doing something that seems to make sense at the time even though later on it doesn't? That was me when I heard that door. Ten to one odds it was just Sully, the janitor, running early on his chores. He's used to seeing me all over the place after school, taking pictures for the school newspaper. Probably wouldn't bat an eye if he found me here. But I was standing at a teacher's desk, looking

through papers. And what if it wasn't Sully?
Deer in the headlights.

Before I even knew what I was doing, I'd
shoved the papers back into the drawer, closed
it, and ducked into the supply closet door in
the back corner.

The supply closet didn't get much use.
All Ms. Opal needed to teach math was the
whiteboard and the laptop she brought in every
day to project slides. The closet collected junk,
mostly—stacks of old textbooks and worn-out
erasers. The place smelled like an attic. I willed
myself not to sneeze and sat on the stepstool
stashed inside the door. I didn't have time to
close the door all the way—I could still see
through a little crack.

Just my luck, I heard bracelets jingling.
That had to be Ms. Opal. I saw a dark-haired
woman take a seat at the desk. Definitely Opal.
Nobody else I could think of had black hair as
long as hers, all the way down her back. She
was sitting just a couple yards away from my

hiding place. Her back was to the closet, so she wasn't likely to see that the door was ajar. But what about that unlocked drawer?

I held my breath, trying not to make a sound. Just as I'd hoped, she unlocked the drawer without trying it first. If she'd been paying attention, she might've realized that the key felt different in the lock. Wrong somehow. But she didn't seem to notice a thing.

She pulled a folder out of the drawer and spread a bunch of papers in front of her. They looked familiar—green ink, rows and rows of circles and pencil marks. Of course—they were the Academic Readiness Assessment tests we'd been taking all week. What was Ms. Opal doing with them?

As I watched, she took a booklet out of the folder and opened it up. She seemed to be comparing the booklet to the test in front of her. Which was weird—teachers don't grade those tests. They get sent to some state facility for scanning. At least that's what I thought.

And then she started changing answers.

I thought my eyes were playing tricks on me at first, but I kept watching. She had an eraser, and she kept using it on parts of the tests, then filling in circles with a pencil.

Ms. Opal was cheating.

I'm not a reporter, but I guess taking so many pictures for the school newspaper and the yearbook has given me a certain mind-set. Once I was sure about what she was doing, I knew I had to document it. Had to record the proof.

I eased my camera out of my backpack, moving just a few inches at a time, keeping a careful grip. I'd had it for a little more than a year—I flipped burgers for an entire summer to buy it. The camera's nothing a pro would use, but it's a sweet little piece of equipment. With the right lens, I can snap a winning basket just as it swishes through the net. Switch up the settings, and I can capture landscapes that would make your jaw drop. Switch 'em up again and I can get spectacular close-ups, which is what I had in mind right then.

To pull that off, though, I'd have to get into the right position. Very slowly, I stood up from the stepstool and mounted it. First rung . . . second rung . . . and the top. The angle wasn't easy to find, focusing on the desk while balancing on the stool. But I had just enough height to be able to zoom in on the test papers, keeping Ms. Opal and her hands in the frame. Lucky for me, the weather had just turned chilly, so the school's ancient heating system was running full blast. It made enough racket that my target didn't hear a thing as the camera clicked.

The toughest part was sitting tight in that closet once I'd gotten my shots. Ms. Opal spent almost an hour going over those tests. The entire time, I had to keep still in this ridiculously small space. One sneeze and I would've been busted. Then again, I probably had nothing to worry about. Ms. Opal was pretty focused on what she was doing. Wouldn't you be?

CHAPTER THREE

It was dark when I finally made it out to my car. First things first: I texted my buddy Vince, who needed that answer key at least as much as I did. *No joy*, I typed. He responded with an impressive string of swear words.

As I drove home, I thought about what I'd seen in Ms. Opal's classroom. Could I have misunderstood what she was doing?

I didn't have a chance to review the evidence until after dinner, when I uploaded the photos to my laptop and enlarged them on the screen. The first couple didn't show anything conclusive, just Opal hunched over the papers on her desk. Then came the ones where I'd used the zoom. The money I invested in the camera had been well spent. You could see everything: the stack of tests with dozens of penciled-in circles; the booklet with the test questions; and right in Opal's hand, an eraser going over someone's answer. The next shot showed her pencil, filling in a different bubble. And so on, over and over, a couple dozen crystal-clear shots.

As far as I could guess, Opal must've taken the test herself and made an answer key. Then she checked our work and fixed some of the wrong answers she found. Even seeing it right there in front of me again, it was hard to believe a teacher would cheat on the standardized tests. They're more than just a way of grading the school. We have to pass them to graduate. Sure, we get multiple tries if we don't pass the first time. But everybody has to pass eventually or no diploma. Plus the teachers get evaluated based on our scores, and that affects their raises and promotions and stuff.

So if Ms. Opal really did change answers on those tests, she was messing with people's futures.

Then again, she'd have to be changing wrong answers to correct ones, right? Otherwise, she'd just be screwing herself, because it'd hurt her if her students failed. So she must have been giving us a boost on the test—kind of like the one I was hoping to give myself on tomorrow's trig exam. Our scores go up, she gets a bigger raise, and we get to graduate. Win-win.

Besides, who was I to judge? I would've cheated on Ms. Opal's exam if I'd found that answer key.

I almost deleted the photos right then and there. But something held me back. Maybe I just needed to stop thinking about it for a little while. After all, I had an awful lot of trigonometry to study.

CHAPTER FOUR

A couple of hours later, as I felt like I couldn't cram one more formula into my tired brain, my cell phone rang out with the Natalie chime. That's the sound my phone makes to ensure I don't miss any of my girlfriend's messages. She always texts me to say good night, and tonight was no exception.

Nat had been pretty busy herself that evening, cheering with the squad. That's how we got together, actually—her cheerleading gig.

I love shooting sports because the challenge never gets old. The position, the angle, the timing, the light—all of them have to come together perfectly to get a decent action shot. But I have to admit, I kind of had a bias against cheerleaders. Still do. I just don't get them. Everybody's already there to watch the team, so why do we need girls in little skirts to get us to yell about it? The whole thing seems like a setup, an excuse for them to wear ridiculous outfits and date jocks.

I probably wouldn't have even noticed Nat if she hadn't fallen on me. I'd been shooting the year's first home game, scrambling down the sideline to find a shot. I guess I ran behind the cheerleaders just as Nat took the top spot in the pyramid. She saw me zip by out of the corner of her eye and lost it. Yes, I was that freaking cute (her words). All I know is that one minute I was in motion. The next, I was on the ground, beneath a girl whose hair smelled like coconuts.

Honestly, after I scrambled to my feet, my first thought was for my camera. No damage. Then I took a look at the girl brushing herself off in front of me, and whoa. Curly hair, green eyes, and something clever in her expression.

"You know," she said, "if this was a movie, I'd have to say something about falling hard for you."

"Uh, right," I said. "Good thing this is just real life, huh?"

I pride myself on knowing how to talk to girls, but all of a sudden I was out of words. So I smiled and asked if she was okay.

She smiled back. "Yeah. But maybe text me later to make sure I don't, you know, have a concussion or anything?"

She gave me her number, just like that. And then she popped back in line with the other girls, shouting something about the superiority of our football players.

That's how it began, with an accident. And in the weeks since, I'd wondered plenty of times if I could ever have a luckier one. Nat turned out to be the real deal, a girl I could laugh with, talk with, party with, even study with.

Anyway, the night after I took photos of Ms. Opal, my first instinct was to send Nat the pics after her text. But I hesitated. Opal wasn't just the most popular teacher at our school. She was also the cheerleading coach.

From what Nat had told me, Ms. Opal was almost like a second mom to the girls on the squad. Helped them out with their personal problems, that kind of thing. Nat pretty much worshipped her. Something told me that my girlfriend would be upset about my discovery, even though I had no intention of being a narc.

It wasn't often that I concealed things from Nat. In fact, this week had been the first time. I hadn't told her I was going to try to steal the answer key to the trig test. But I guess there's a second time for everything. I texted back good night and kept my secret to myself.

CHAPTER FIVE

The next morning, I met up with Vince before the first bell. He looked as tired as I felt.

"Up late studying?" I asked.

He nodded. "I can't believe Opal's giving this exam right after three days of state testing. That's just mean, you know?"

I was about to tell him what I'd seen from the supply closet, but as we rounded a corner, we walked right into Kevin Scofield. Kevin thinks he's this dangerous guy, but he's all talk.

"Well, look who's here," he said. "Sushi and Fairy."

Sushi was for me. Very original, right? And

Fairy was for Vince. Even less original.

Vince made a big show of looking over his shoulder, trying to see his back. "Seriously? Did I grow wings or something?"

Wilson High School has something like six students who are out. That's six out of eight hundred. Vince was the first, back in middle school. But he and I have been best friends way longer than that—since third grade, when we were desk buddies in art class. We made a giant clay sculpture of a T. rex. It probably would've gotten a killer grade if the assignment hadn't been to make a model of a ship.

"They're probably under your shirt, sweetie," Kevin said. "How about we take a look?"

"Excuse me, boys." It was Sully, the janitor, pushing his dust mop toward us. Vince and I stepped aside. Kevin stood his ground, of course. Sully had to go around him.

"Make sure to get that fairy dust over there, Mr. Janitor." Kevin pointed toward Vince's feet.

"Dude," I said, "the man has a name. And

you really need to work on your routine. You can steal your material from TV for a while, but eventually you gotta step it up."

Sully cracked a grin. Kevin muttered something and stomped off. I gave him props for that excellent comeback. Vince ducked into the restroom as I went on to class, hoping I'd be half as clever on the test as I'd just been with Kevin the bigot.

No such luck. The trig test turned out to be even harder than I expected. You could hear the pencils flying as all thirty of us scratched away at the problems Opal had inflicted on us. I figured I'd be lucky if I finished it before the bell rang.

"Vincent," Ms. Opal said out of nowhere. Her voice sounded harder than I'd ever heard it. "Stand up and show me your hand."

As Vince obeyed, a chorus of *oohs* started up. From my seat, I could see the ink covering his palm. It looked like he'd copied down a few formulas when he made that stop in the restroom before class. Uh-oh.

Vince knew he was totally busted. He didn't even try to deny anything, just handed the test paper to Ms. Opal with his head hanging low.

"I will not tolerate cheating," Ms. Opal said firmly.

Oh, really?

"You can head to the principal's office," she added. "I'll see you there after class."

Vince grabbed his stuff and slouched out of the room, his face carefully set in an expression of indifference.

Dang. If only I'd found that answer key, Vince wouldn't have resorted to such a stupid trick. Opal had some nerve, busting my friend for something she'd done herself the day before in the same classroom. Cheating is cheating, right? Vince wanted to up his grade. Opal wanted to up our scores to make herself look better. I didn't see much difference.

After that, the test just didn't hold my attention. Vince would probably get in some serious trouble over this. Couldn't Opal have just pulled him aside after class? Maybe make him retake the test instead of sending him to see Juarez? It's not like Vince was a troublemaker or a repeat offender. He just made a bad choice—one bad choice. Now it would probably end up on his permanent record.

I didn't see Vince again until lunch. Turned out he got two weeks of detention. Plus a zero on the test, of course.

At first, he just laughed it off. "My own stupid fault," he said between tater tots. "I should've known I'd get caught. The really annoying thing is I just know I'm gonna get grounded."

"Dude," I said. "You'll miss Marco's party."

"Yeah, I know."

Marco Salinas throws a truly awesome bash every Halloween. He turns his whole place into a haunted house. Plus there's a ridiculous amount of "treats" of various kinds. Tomorrow was the big night. Nat and I had been looking forward to it for weeks. Vince too.

I told Vince about my discovery the day before. He quit laughing things off then and got really quiet.

"That's . . . interesting," he finally said. "I'll be sure to ponder that while I'm cooling my heels in detention. And while my parents yell at me. And ground me and whatever else they can think of."

"Sucks, man," I said. "Busting you the way she did."

He nodded. We didn't talk much after that, just ate our food and went on to class.

* * *

After school, I drove to Simmons Park to take some pictures. The park is mostly baseball diamonds and soccer fields, but there's this one section that actually feels like real woods, thick with oaks and maples. At the end of October, the fall colors start to dull a bit. I wasn't there to photograph leaves, though. I was there for the creek.

I followed the trail that led to the water's edge and listened to the sounds for a minute. The water moved slowly, like it didn't really have anywhere to go but wanted to wander a bit anyway. I could hear it burbling here and there over rocks and fallen branches.

I've been photographing this spot for four months, since the summer solstice. That's the longest day of the year, when the light is brightest and strongest. Every week or so I come by and take the same shot of the water— same position, same perspective, same time of day. The shadows and reflections are just a little bit different each time, changing as the seasons advance. It probably sounds weird, I know. But it amazes me, the way these tiny changes make every photo different from the one before it.

I set myself up to record this week's shots, but something wasn't right. I couldn't relax into the rhythm of it like I usually do. I kept thinking about Ms. Opal and Vince and those stupid tests. My shots came out all kinds of weird—too much glare, out of focus, just wrong. Finally, I packed it in and trudged back to my car.

By the time I got home, I knew exactly what I needed to do. I fired up my laptop and went to the school newspaper's website. It's set up like a blog with password protection—only the editors can post. I happen to be the photo editor, a position I'd never fully appreciated until that moment.

I typed for a half hour without stopping. Then I uploaded three choice photographs. And then I clicked the Publish button and refreshed the page.

WWHS Teacher Caught Cheating
by Kai Tamura
Earlier this week, I took the photos you see here of Ms. Michelle Opal, WWHS math teacher

and cheerleading coach. I personally witnessed Ms. Opal changing answers on numerous copies of the Academic Readiness Assessment (ARA). As this newspaper has previously reported, the school district evaluates teachers based on student scores on this test. Pay raises are tied to the percentage of students who achieve a passing grade.

For obvious reasons, I did not confront Ms. Opal with my discovery at the time I took these photographs. If she would like to comment on her actions, I'll update this post accordingly. For now, we can only wonder why a teacher who says she won't tolerate cheating would engage in this dishonest practice herself.

I posted a link to the story on Instagram, then tweeted it (*#cheater, #TeacherBusted, #OhNoSheDidnt*). There'd be no shortage of hits on my article in the next few hours. That was for sure.

CHAPTER SIX

I'll admit I felt pretty nervous heading to my trig class the next morning. Would Ms. Opal even be there? Maybe Principal Juarez would've already read the story and pulled her out of class to talk about what had happened. I hoped so. Somehow I couldn't quite imagine facing her in front of everybody.

No such luck. Ms. Opal was there as usual, setting up the day's slide show on her laptop. She seemed totally calm. Didn't even look up as I walked in. That's when it hit me: she didn't know about the story yet. It's not like any teachers follow me on social media, you know?

The older generation would need a little time to catch up with recent events.

My classmates were a different story, though. Everybody was whispering, looking at me, looking at Ms. Opal, looking back at me again. A couple of girls glared at me—cheerleaders. Not a great sign for the conversation I planned to have with Nat after class. But most people were just grinning, hoping for drama. You could've sold a lot of popcorn in that room.

Vince looked like he'd won the lottery. The minute I took my seat, he stood up and starting bowing the "I'm not worthy" bow. Laughter spread around the classroom. Then the bell rang, Ms. Opal shushed everyone, and we settled in for forty-five minutes of tangents and cosines.

* * *

After trig, I found Nat at her locker. I could tell from the expression on her face that my experiment in online journalism wasn't sitting too well with her.

"Hey, beautiful," I said, leaning in to kiss her. "You okay?"

She stepped away and folded her arms across her chest.

"Do you know what people are *saying*?"

"Um, that I'm the greatest photographer in the history of Woodrow Wilson High School?" I tried again to give her a kiss, but she wasn't having any of it.

"They're saying you faked those photos to get Ms. Opal in trouble," she said.

"Huh? Why would I do that?" I said. I wanted to sound casual, but it came out touchy instead. Defensive.

"Because she busted your best friend for cheating."

"No," I said. "No way. I didn't fake the pics. She really did change the answers on those tests." I tried to keep my voice level, but I felt my stomach flip-flopping.

She looked away. "I don't know if I believe you."

"I wouldn't lie to you."

"Even if the pics are real, why'd you have to post them?" she asked. "You could've kept it a secret."

Now we were getting down to business. Nat thought Opal should've gotten a pass on her cheating because everyone likes her. Of course, I pretty much thought the same thing until she busted Vince.

I tried to explain. "She's got one standard for herself and another for her students. It's not right. She flunked Vince on that test and reported him to the principal when she'd just cheated herself."

"Oh," Nat said. "So you *did* post the pics because she busted your friend."

"That's not what I meant." This was going all wrong.

She shrugged. "Whatever, Kai. I'll meet you at the party tonight, okay?"

"You don't want me to pick you up?"

"No, I'm going with some girls from the squad. I'll see you there." And with that obvious dismissal, she left me standing by her locker.

How could Nat think I could do something so nasty? I mean, I'm not a perfect human being, but I'm not a jerk. She should know me better than that, I thought.

I went to my next class, US history. People were still talking—I could tell from how they kept looking at me and whispering. But I didn't feel any kind of satisfaction anymore. After my conversation with Nat, I kept imagining my classmates were calling me a liar, a faker.

Vince found me on the way to lunch. "Your article's gone," he said. "The photos too. The administration must've pulled them off the website."

"I'm surprised it took them this long."

"So much for free speech, am I right?" He stopped in his tracks and pointed. "Whoa.

Looks like they didn't pull your article quite fast enough."

A camera crew had set up in the lobby, right outside the cafeteria. A reporter spoke into a microphone while holding up a huge printout of one of my photos. And right beside him, looking royally mad, stood Ms. Opal.

CHAPTER SEVEN

For a second, I wanted to duck into the cafeteria and pretend I hadn't seen the news crew. I like being behind the camera, not in front of it. Besides, the whole situation was starting to get out of control. But Vince pushed me toward the reporter.

"Don't let them tell just her side of the story. You've gotta talk to them too."

Ms. Opal's eyes narrowed as we approached. The reporter turned to see who she was glaring at.

"Are you Kai Tamura?" he asked. He sounded like he'd just won a prize. "The student who took this photo?"

The reporter waved his printout in my face like a flag. He also turned my way, leaving Ms. Opal out of the picture. She started to say something, but I cut in first.

"Yes, I'm Kai Tamura, and I took that photo and posted it to our school newspaper's website."

The reporter beamed. "You've made some serious allegations about your teacher, Kai. Do you stand by those charges?"

I reminded myself to look at the camera as I spoke into the mike. "Absolutely. I know what I saw."

"Why do you think Ms. Opal committed this alleged act of cheating?"

"You'll have to ask her that. Like I wrote in the article, my guess is that she wanted to make sure she would get a good performance review. And a good raise."

"And why do you think the administration removed your article and photos from the website?"

"I don't know, maybe they're afraid of the

truth coming out?" I said. "And maybe they don't want people talking about whether it's fair to give teachers raises based on students' test scores."

"Kai, tell us how you ended up taking those photos in the first place."

Uh-oh. I should have been prepared for a question like this, but I wasn't.

"Well," I began, stalling for time. "I was in the classroom because—"

A voice cut in from down the hallway. "Stop! Stop filming immediately!"

It was Principal Juarez, a man I'd never been happy to see until that moment. He charged down the hall toward the cameraman, waving his arms like it was a national crisis.

"This is an educational institution! It is not open to reporters during the school day."

I wondered if that was true. Schools are public places, right? But I guess the administration can keep you out if you don't have official business there.

The reporter jumped on his chance. "Principal Juarez, would you care to comment on—"

Juarez reached the camera and put his hand over the lens. "You will vacate these premises immediately." He looked around, his voice jumping up an octave. "Security!"

The reporter seemed to know that his opportunity had passed. "Of course, sir. No problem. We'll be on our way." He told the cameraman to pack it up.

Juarez relaxed. "Kai, please join me in my office."

The reporter raised his eyebrows, looking intrigued, but Juarez told him not to push his luck. Then he turned to me again. "*Now*, Kai," he said, as if I was somehow stalling.

I glanced back at Vince as I followed the principal. His expression mirrored what I felt exactly:

Oh, crap.

CHAPTER EIGHT

Thirty minutes later, I was suspended. Never mind that Juarez had absolutely no proof that I'd faked the pics. Never mind that it would have been incredibly difficult to fake them in the first place. You'd have to be a genius with Photoshop—I didn't even know how to use it. It was a teacher's word against mine. Not even photographic evidence could make the difference in that contest.

As I drove home, I tried to figure out when my parents would hear from Juarez about my punishment. He could call them at work, which would mean they'd know before I even got to talk to them. But he'd said he would talk to them in the evening—and that I should prepare them for the call. If he kept his word, I should have a few hours to figure out how to make my case.

Then I remembered the news crew. The local news might just beat Juarez to the punch if Mom or Dad came home in time to watch it. Or if any of their friends saw it and called them to tell them. But that reporter didn't know I'd been suspended. At least, I didn't think he did.

And then I remembered one more thing: It was Friday. Marco's big Halloween bash was tonight. Not that I felt like partying, but Nat had said she would meet me there. And this did not seem like the right time to stand up my girlfriend. Not after our conversation that morning.

The party didn't start till seven, but my parents would be home way before then. I'd need to explain to them what had happened before they heard Juarez's version. But if I touched base with Mom and Dad, there was pretty much no chance I'd be going to the Halloween party. My parents are reasonable, usually, but even if they believed my version of events, they'd want to know the same thing that reporter had asked: How had I ended up taking the photos in the first place? And why did I post them online instead of taking them to Juarez?

No matter what I came up with to explain my presence in that supply closet, I couldn't see any way I'd avoid getting grounded, at least for as long as I was suspended from school. That would mean no party and no chance to see Nat, maybe for days.

Once I got home, I checked the website of the local news station that had been at school. They'd already posted a story. The headline made my stomach lurch: *WILSON HIGH SCHOOL STUDENT DOCTORS PHOTOS OF TEACHER*

My interview was there too, but the

reporter followed it up by noting that school officials had taken disciplinary measures.

When my parents saw this, they would go nuts.

I made up my mind. No waiting around for the inevitable. This was my last chance to determine my own fate for a while.

I wrote my parents a note and left it on the kitchen table:

> *Mom and Dad,*
> *Tonight you'll hear from Principal Juarez about some things he claims I did. Please remember there's another side to this story. I didn't do anything wrong. Will explain when I get home later.*
> *Love you both,*
> *Kai*

Then I threw my Halloween costume in the car and drove to a coffee shop. Three hours to go till the party, but I wasn't taking a chance on staying home.

CHAPTER NINE

I spent the next couple hours on my phone, playing games and generally killing time. I texted Nat but didn't hear back. She had cheerleading practice, though, so that wasn't too strange. Vince checked in to see what had happened with Juarez. Turned out he was right about getting grounded.

Dude, I texted back, *u won't be the only 1 by the time my parents are done w/me.*

Finally, seven o'clock rolled around. I grabbed a burger and drove over to Marco's. My costume was simple enough to put on in the car, no problem. Nat and I were both going as pirates. I secretly thought it was a kind of boring idea, but she wanted something that we could do as a couple. So I'd put together the usual gear: wooden sword, eye patch, vest, bandana tied on my head, some cool lace-up boots I'd found at a thrift store. I'd even practiced saying "Arrr!" and making puns about booty and buried treasure.

I was ready. Now all I needed was my lovely shipmate.

Trouble was, Nat wasn't on the scene. I toured Marco's house and backyard, eyes peeled. I saw three fairies, two butterflies, a ladybug, a nurse, and a startling number of sexy vampires, but no pirate girl. So I chilled with some guys from the photography club for a while, then texted Nat again.

"Hey, Captain Sushi! Arrr!" A guy in an Iron Man mask punched me in the arm—not in a friendly way. I didn't need to see under the mask to know it was Kevin Scofield. I stomped away before he started making cracks about my missing first mate.

Another ten minutes passed before my cell phone sounded the Natalie chime. Her text was in all caps. Not a good sign.

CAN'T MAKE IT, SRRY

Why not?

I REALLY DON'T FEEL LIKE PARTYING WHEN THE WHOLE SQUAD IS MAD @ ME. THX 4 THAT BTW.

So Natalie was upset that my exposé had hurt her social standing. Great.

If there's one thing I can't stand, it's arguing by text. Take one angry person, add another, and force them both to type it all out, one line at a time. Yeah, there's no possible way *that* could go wrong. My usual policy is to stop texting the minute I start feeling annoyed with someone.

But I was too—well, too annoyed to remember that right then.

I didn't mean 4 that 2 happen, I texted back.

EVRY1 SAYS MY BF BACKSTABBED

OUR COACH N NOW SHE'LL BE FIRED

She's not getting fired. I got suspended. I'm fine tho, thx 4 askin

UR SUSPENDED???

Yeah, 1 week

SO U DID FAKE THOSE PIX

No! I already told u I didn't. But Juarez doesn't believe me.

I DON'T BELIEVE U EITHER

Fine, don't. Still tru.

U DON'T GET SUSPENDED 4 DOIN NOTHIN WRONG

Um, I just did

U FAKED THE PIX 2 GET BACK AT HER. JUST ADMIT IT KAI.

We shld talk F2F, let me come pick u up.

4GET IT. IM DONE WITH U.

Nat. Come on.

Nat???

She didn't answer. I called, but she didn't pick up. Left a message, but—you got it—she didn't call back.

I tried to process what had just happened. My girlfriend—my gorgeous, funny girlfriend—had just dumped me. By text message. Over a few photographs. Not even sexy photos of some other girl or something. A few very boring photos of a math teacher with an eraser in her hand.

It was starting to suck to be me.

CHAPTER TEN

I left the party early and went home. My parents met me at the door as if they'd been standing there all night.

Right away, I knew things were about to go from bad to worse. I'd never seen my dad so angry.

"Kaito!" he said. "Sit down."

I took a seat in the kitchen and pulled the bandana off my head. "I know what you're thinking," I began, "but you don't know the whole story—"

"We know you lied, you falsely accused a teacher, you doctored photographs," Dad said.

Mom jumped in. "You got suspended. Suspended! And then you went to that party without even telling us about it."

"Do you have any idea how humiliating it was when your principal called to talk with us?" my father said. "Having to admit to a school official that we had no idea what was going on with our own son?"

Wow. They didn't even want to hear my side of the story. They were too busy tag teaming me to care.

". . . your permanent record!" Mom was saying. "Every college you apply to will find out about this."

"And your name is in the local news," Dad said. "This is part of your digital footprint now. And do you realize we could be sued by your teacher for defamation of character?"

Sued? For telling the truth? I didn't think so. But what did I know? I was just the person who took the photos. Clearly the adults had all the answers here.

Dad doesn't yell much, but when he gets going, look out. By the time he ran out of steam, my mom was crying, and I had pretty much stopped listening.

They grounded me, of course, "until further notice." Mom promised a long list of chores for me to do during my suspension, and Dad told me I was lucky he didn't take away my camera. I started to argue that point. (The camera is mine. I paid for it with my own money.) But I realized I'd better not push it.

I had to say something, though. "You forgot to go over the part where you don't need to hear my version of all this because obviously I can't be trusted," I said. "And the part where you're sure the principal got everything right because school officials never screw over students. Or make mistakes."

I let that sink in for a minute, then stomped to my room. I was finished letting everyone else tell me their version of what I'd done. It was time to take back control of the story.

CHAPTER ELEVEN

I'll say this for my parents: They can be jerks, but they're not total jerks. When I get grounded, I can keep my phone and my laptop. I can still go online too. I spent the next couple hours doing research. There had to be a way of proving that I hadn't doctored those photos. If I could just get Principal Juarez to believe me on that point, he'd have no choice but to admit that Ms. Opal really had cheated.

Turns out there's an entire branch of forensics devoted to this stuff. I always thought of forensics as crime-scene analysis, like you see on TV: blood spatters, hair, DNA, that kind of thing. But digital forensics is all about getting evidence from computers, phones, tablets—and digital cameras.

Digital forensics technicians can trace and recover e-mails, device locations, text message histories, you name it. Stuff you think you've deleted is almost always still in your device, buried somewhere. And the technicians can analyze photos to see whether they've been manipulated. Cutting-edge stuff, not easy to do but possible.

A little more digging turned up three companies in the state that specialized in digital forensics. Two of them were a hundred miles away. But the third, McNamara Digital Forensics, had an office in my town. Their website specifically mentioned image analysis. Jackpot.

I went to bed at one in the morning, feeling hopeful. But I couldn't fall asleep. I kept picturing Nat the way I'd last seen her, avoiding my gaze like she didn't even know me. I guess she didn't—at least not the way I thought she did. Was it wrong to expect her to believe me, no matter what she thought about Ms. Opal? No matter what her cheerleader friends said about me?

I tried to imagine what I would think if things were the other way around. What if Nat was telling me something I couldn't quite believe? Would I have trusted her? I thought so. I hoped so. What if Vince told me she was lying, though? What then?

I didn't know for sure. I'd known Vince a lot longer than I'd known Nat—years longer. Sure, I was crazy about Nat, but I trusted Vince like nobody else in the world. It would be hard to ignore him if he had a strong belief about something important.

But would I just dump Nat without even hearing her out? And by text? No. I'd never do that, no matter what she did.

Maybe, if I could prove my innocence, Nat would change her mind about me. But either way, something had shifted between us.

After tossing and turning for I don't know how long, I finally drifted off. I dreamed about the news reporter interviewing my parents. My dad said he'd never had such a disappointing son. (That didn't make sense because I'm his only kid, but that's dreamland for you.) And my mom sang a song about swimming in circles.

I woke up at five o'clock, more tired than I'd been the night before. I had a feeling I wouldn't be getting much rest until all this was over.

CHAPTER TWELVE

I spent the weekend cleaning out the garage and the basement—washing the walls, mopping, everything. By Monday morning, I'd finished the monster list of chores my mom had hoped would keep me busy for my whole suspension. After my dad left for work, I went to the website of McNamara Digital Forensics and set up a video chat appointment with a technician.

At ten o'clock, I logged on. The technician wasn't quite what I expected. I guess I was picturing a nerdy guy, but it turned out to be a green-haired girl named Charlotte. She looked to be around twenty and had piercings in her nose, eyebrow, and lip, plus about eight in her ears. You know how piercings are butt-ugly on some people but kind of sexy on others? I've never quite figured out what makes the difference. Well, on Charlotte they were hot.

I jumped right in and explained my situation. I even admitted that I'd gotten suspended and I was trying to clear myself.

"Well," Charlotte said, "we can examine your photos, sure. But our report isn't going to clear you unless the evidence shows the photos weren't altered."

"That's good," I said quickly. "That's just what I want. No bias either way."

She smiled. "You know, I think I saw a story about you on the news last night. Did you do an interview?"

I wasn't sure how to respond to that. "Um, yeah. There was a news crew at school before I got suspended."

"You have a good presence on camera," she said. "Very confident."

"Well, nobody seems to believe me, whether I looked confident or not."

Charlotte nodded. "I know what that's like." Then she got back to business. "Our fee is $150 per hour, billed by the quarter hour. Your three photos will probably require an hour or so apiece. So with taxes, it'll come to around 500. We'll need a deposit of $150 to get started. We'll bill you for the rest when we deliver our report."

I tried to keep a straight face. Five hundred bucks? My bank account had maybe three hundred, tops.

Breathe, Kai, I thought. *You can figure this out.*

"Do you guys have, like, a payment plan or anything?" I could feel my face turning red. It was a good thing I wasn't trying to impress the green-haired girl, because I'd be toast.

She didn't get snarky, though. Her face kind of softened.

"You know what? Let me check with my boss about that. He's a good guy. I bet we can work something out."

"Thanks, that'd be great."

Charlotte told me the best way for them to proceed would be to pull the original images from my camera's internal memory. "That way, we can confirm that we're working with the exact photos you took, and then we can compare those files to the ones you posted online."

I couldn't quite bring myself to admit that I couldn't leave my house because I was grounded. I told Charlotte it would take me a couple of hours to get there, and we signed off.

On a typical weekday, sneaking out while grounded wouldn't be that hard. My dad works the usual Monday-Friday schedule at his accounting job, and my mom is full-time at the library. But just my luck, she'd worked over the weekend, and today was her day off. So I had to figure out how to slip out under my mom's nose, walk three miles to McNamara Digital Forensics, and get back inside the house before Mom realized I was gone.

Pretty unlikely. I decided to start with a more direct approach.

"Would it be okay if I did some errands today, Mom?"

She looked at me as if I'd lost my mind. "Kaito, what part of being grounded do you not understand?"

"Yeah, I know, it's just—I need some stuff for a school project. So I don't fall too far behind."

She raised her eyebrows. "What kind of project?"

"Well, for biology we have to make, like, a mock science fair project? And Mr. Moynihan's going to pick the best ones to send to the actual science fair. You know, the statewide one where the winners get scholarships."

That caught her attention. "So you need supplies? What's your project going to be?"

"Well, Vince and I are partners. He has a pet rat. You remember me telling you about her? Constance."

Mom wrinkled her nose. "Not really."

"Yeah, she's really smart. We're gonna build a maze and get a mouse and a gerbil and compare them to the rat to see which one can learn the maze the fastest. So I need to go to the hardware store to get supplies for the maze."

"I don't want any rodents in my house, Kaito."

"Right, I know. We're gonna keep the animals at Vince's place. And I'll build the maze here and bring it over there so we can train them."

Mom still looked doubtful. "Well," she said, "since you've finished your chores already, I guess schoolwork is the next best way for you to spend your suspension. But you'll go to the hardware store and come straight back. Is that understood?"

"Yeah, of course. Absolutely."

As I drove to McNamara Digital Forensics with my camera concealed under my jacket, I tried not to feel too guilty. Vince does have a rat named Constance, so at least that part was true.

CHAPTER THIRTEEN

Charlotte sat behind a desk in a small lobby, typing away at a computer. She smiled when she saw me.

"Good news," she said. "Bob—that's my boss—says we can set up a payment plan for you as long as you make the initial $150 deposit."

"That I can do," I said.

"Nice camera," she observed as I handed it to her. "You must have spent a fortune on it."

I felt myself blushing. Yeah, I was the guy who had fancy toys but needed a payment plan to purchase her company's services.

"Oh, crikey!" she said when she saw my face. "I didn't mean it that way. Gah, I'm such a . . ."

"Did you just say crikey?"

"I did." She grinned, and her face went all dimply. I have to admit, it was pretty adorable.

"That's, uh, a good word."

"It is, isn't it? So I'll just need you to fill out this form here. It details the work you want done and gives us permission to raid your camera for data. Sign at the bottom."

I filled out the form, requesting that copies of the report be e-mailed to me and to Principal Juarez. Charlotte ran the deposit on my debit card.

"When will you have the report? Do you know?" I asked.

"Five to seven business days."

Uh-oh. That was way too long for my purposes.

"Is there any way you could rush it? I really, really need the report by midday Friday."

"Ten percent rush fee," Charlotte said. "We can fold it into your payment plan."

"Sweet. Thank you so much. You have no idea what this means to me."

She tucked a green curl behind her ear. "Let's just hope we find what you think we will," she said.

At least *that* was one thing I didn't have to worry about.

. . .

The next day, Tuesday, Mom had the day off again. That posed a problem, because I had a second mission to complete. There was no way she would believe another story about needing to run errands. She'd already surveyed my "maze supplies" with a critical eye, trying to figure out if I'd been playing her. (*Note to self*, I'd thought. *Build maze soon.*)

My best bet would be to go while Mom was at her yoga class. During the couple of hours she was out, I'd have plenty of time to drive to school, meet the person I needed to see—hopefully without getting spotted by any faculty members—and get back home.

I wasn't sure what to do with my cell phone. My parents installed one of those annoying GPS trackers on it. ("For your own safety, Kaito," my dad said. Yeah, thanks for the trust, man.) Yesterday, I'd gone to a hardware store on the same block as McNamara Digital Forensics, so that was no problem. But if I took my phone with me today and my parents checked the tracker, I'd be busted.

What if I left the phone behind? If they called or texted to check up on me, that would look bad too. Ultimately, I decided the second problem would be the easier one to deal with. I'd just say the battery had run down and I hadn't noticed.

Nothing could go smoothly for me during my suspension, though. Mom informed me that she was skipping yoga so she could paint the garage (translation: keep an eye on me).

There was no way I could just wander out the front door, much less take my car. I'd have to sneak out, and I'd have to walk. If she checked up on me while I was away, I'd be screwed, but I couldn't do anything about that.

I decided my best shot at getting away unnoticed was to go out my window. Good thing our house is just one story. After Mom started painting, I unlocked the window, pushed it up as far as it would go, and popped out the screen. Then I swung a leg over the sill and tried to figure out what to do next. These things look so easy in the movies, you know? But in real life, it's kind of awkward to climb out a window aboveground, especially if you'd rather not fall into the bushes below.

Okay, so my future career as a ninja wasn't looking so good. Another reason to focus on photography. Finally, I leaped for it, landed with an *oof*, and dusted myself off. My room would be plenty cold by the time I got back, but that was the least of my worries.

It took a half hour to walk to school. I got there in the middle of third period, so the halls were mostly empty. Just in case, I kept my hoodie pulled up after I slipped inside. I traced a route that avoided the administrative offices too. A couple of juniors saw me at one point, but no teachers. So far, so good.

The person I needed to see could have been almost anywhere, so I waited in the one spot I knew he'd come back to eventually. He looked surprised to see me, but he smiled.

"Hey there, photographer Kai," he said. "I heard you were suspended. Whatcha doin' here?"

* * *

If getting out of the window had been tricky, getting back in proved almost impossible. Even in our one-story house, the sill was way above my head. I'm no wimp, but I'm not exactly the pull-up champion of the world. As I scrabbled up and over the sill, I pictured my mom on the other side, ready to scream her head off. But my room was empty, door closed, just like I'd left it.

I put the screen back in place, shut and locked the window, and got a drink of water. Then I headed out to the garage. My mom would probably appreciate some help with that painting.

CHAPTER FOURTEEN

Charlotte didn't let me down. I got my report around four o'clock on Thursday—half a day early. Just as I expected, the findings backed up my story. The photos I'd posted online matched the originals from the camera. They hadn't been altered in any way, just as I'd told Principal Juarez. The thought of him getting the same report in his e-mail and puzzling through it gave me the biggest grin I'd smiled for days.

The next day, I wasn't due at Juarez's office until one o'clock, but I showed up early just in case. I'd dressed to impress in a button-down shirt and slacks. I even made sure my hair looked a bit less wild than usual. I couldn't leave anything to chance.

Juarez greeted me with a much more respectful tone than the one he'd used at our last meeting. I looked him in the eye and put on my "friendly, mature young man" face. Ms. Opal, on the other hand, wouldn't even look at me. She took a seat across from me and directed all her attention to Juarez.

"I've called this meeting so that the two of you can talk through this difficult situation," the principal began. His secretary set down a plastic cup of water in front of each of us, then took a seat off to the side so that she could take notes.

Ms. Opal raised her eyebrows. "My understanding was that you called this meeting so that Kai could apologize to me before being allowed to return to school," she said. Then she faced me for the first time. "I'm listening."

I met her gaze. She looked so offended, so injured, that for a second I wondered if maybe I *did* owe her an apology. But only for a second.

"I stand by my story, Ms. Opal. I know what I saw. And I have proof that I didn't manipulate the photos I took in any way."

"I'm sure Principal Juarez would like to see that proof," Ms. Opal said. "I know I would."

Whoa. Juarez hadn't even told her about the photo analysis—he'd let her walk into the meeting thinking she'd gotten away with the whole thing. Talk about setting someone up for a hard fall. Note to self: Try to stay on the principal's good side from now on.

Juarez cut in. "Actually, I've seen it already. Kai has enlisted the services of a digital forensics team. They've submitted a report that verifies the authenticity of the photos."

I took a printout of the report from my backpack and handed it to Opal. She glanced at it, then tossed it aside. "This could have been faked, just like the photos."

"I thought of that as well, of course," Juarez said. "That's why I've asked the technician who did the work to join us by video chat." He positioned his laptop so that both he and Opal could see the screen. I moved my chair so that I could see too. Juarez opened the chat window, and soon there was Charlotte, saying good afternoon.

"Now, Charlotte," Juarez said in the special talk-down-to-you tone he used with anyone under the age of thirty. "I have your report here, and I understand that you've authenticated these photographs Kai took of his teacher. Is that correct?"

Charlotte smiled helpfully. "Yes, sir." She started to say more, but Juarez cut her off.

"That's all well and good," he said, "but what I really need is confirmation from your manager. Mr., uh, McNamara, is it? Is he available?"

"Oh," Charlotte said. "Sure. I'll get him right away."

I said a silent prayer that McNamara would be at least thirty-five and wouldn't have green (or blue or yellow) hair. Or piercings. Turned out he looked like my dad, only white: a middle-aged, balding dude in a shirt and a tie. In other words, the man oozed respectability. Perfect.

Charlotte introduced him, then stepped out of view of the webcam so that her boss could take the stage. He and Juarez got down to business.

"Mr. McNamara, did you examine the images in question?"

"I did. Charlotte's a reliable technician, but I verify her findings for all our customers. Standard procedure."

"And did you find that the photos had been digitally altered in any way? Photoshopped, anything added or changed?" Juarez looked so proud of himself, using what he probably thought was fancy technospeak.

"Not at all. We have the ability to analyze the metadata of JPEG files like these to determine—"

"Fine, fine," Juarez said. "So you can confirm that the photos are authentic, is that what I'm hearing?" He sounded like a prosecutor at a trial. No, more like a judge.

"Absolutely."

"Wait a minute," Ms. Opal interrupted. "Kai is this man's customer. How do we know we're getting an honest assessment, not one that Kai paid for?"

I raised my eyebrows and offered my most innocent expression.

"My services are trusted by police departments across the state," McNamara said. "I have an endorsement from the local district attorney and another from the sheriff's department. Please be assured that—"

"Yes, all right," Juarez said. "Please, Mr. McNamara, I understand where you're coming from. Thank you so much for your time."

Just as they signed off, someone knocked at the door, then opened it. The janitor poked his head in.

"Mr. Sullivan?" Juarez said. "Is there some problem?"

"Actually, sir," I said, "I asked Sully—Mr. Sullivan—to come by. He has something important to tell you."

Sully took a chair across from Opal and Juarez.

Juarez frowned. I imagined he didn't like losing control of his courtroom, even for a moment. "What's this about?" he said. "Kai, please fill us in."

This was it. Time for the final act. "Well, like I said last week, I was hiding in the supply closet when I took the photos of Ms. Opal," I began. "And while I was in there, I heard the classroom door open, and then I heard Mr. Sullivan saying hello."

Opal looked surprised, then confused, then angry. She started to speak, but Juarez held up a hand. "What happened next, Kai?" he said.

I made sure to sound as natural as I could. Not rehearsed at all. "I, um, I heard Ms. Opal tell Mr. Sullivan to get out. She said the room didn't need cleaning and she was busy. And then Mr. Sullivan said sorry, good night, and I heard the door open and shut again."

Opal couldn't keep quiet any longer. "This is ridiculous!" she said. "This is a complete lie."

Juarez shushed her again. "Mr. Sullivan," he said, "what did you see when you entered the classroom on the day in question?"

I held my breath. Everything hung on this moment.

Sully cleared his throat. "Well, it was like this," he began. "I opened the door and rolled my stuff inside—"

"Yes, yes," Juarez said.

"And Ms. Opal, she had all these papers spread out on her desk and an eraser in her hand and she was bent over one of the green papers. And then she looked up and saw me and just about bit my head off."

Ms. Opal stood up. "Never! I never did any of that!"

"Now, Kai," Juarez said. "This would have been very helpful information to have last week, when I first confronted you about these photographs. Why didn't you mention Mr. Sullivan's visit to the classroom then?"

I'd prepared for this question too. "Honestly, sir, I didn't even think about it at the time. Everything was happening so fast. I was in shock that Ms. Opal would accuse me of doctoring the photos. It didn't occur to me until the next day that I had a witness who could back me up, and by then I was suspended."

Ms. Opal stood up. "You lying little—"

"That's enough!" Juarez said. "You've told your side of the story, Michelle. The facts aren't backing you up." He turned to me. "Kai, there's one question you still haven't answered. What were you doing in that closet?"

I gave a sheepish smile. "It's kind of embarrassing, sir. I lost my trig textbook, and I was hoping to find another one without bugging Ms. Opal."

Juarez nodded. "Well, that explains it. Kai,

part of being a leader is admitting it when you make a mistake. I made a mistake here, and I apologize to you."

I started to croak out a "thank you," but Juarez was too caught up in the moment. He just kept talking.

"I'm scrubbing the suspension from your record," he said. "We can question your judgment in publishing the photos the way you did, but no one can question your intentions. You have my thanks for protecting the integrity of our school and our testing process. And thank you, Mr. Sullivan, for helping to clarify the situation."

I managed to squeeze in a few words. "So my suspension is over?"

"Officially, it never happened. We'll look forward to seeing you back in class tomorrow morning."

And with that, he stood up. Court now in recess.

"Oh," he added, "I'll be certain to phone

your parents tonight and explain the entire situation to them. They deserve an apology as well."

"Thank you so much, Principal Juarez. And thank you for keeping an open mind." I almost made myself puke with that last bit. It was so fake. But the situation clearly demanded some butt kissing.

Ms. Opal looked like she might lose it. She started to get up, but Juarez gestured again with his hand: Sit down. Looked like the sentencing phase was about to begin.

Out in the corridor, I thanked Sully for backing me up. He flashed a grin and told me to take it easy.

And just like that, I was redeemed. Proved innocent. Forgiven—at least, as far as the system was concerned.

CHAPTER FIFTEEN

On my way home, I stopped by McNamara Digital Forensics to pick up my camera.

"Did everything work out?" Charlotte asked. "Things were getting pretty dramatic from what I could hear."

I filled her in, and we laughed at the idea that her boss would fake a report for a few hundred bucks from a high school student. I noticed a pile of textbooks on her desk, which gave me a good opening to ask where she went to school.

"I'm at the tech college for now," she said. "My second year, studying digital forensics.

One of the cool things about this job is that I can study when business is slow."

"Nice."

"Yeah. So you're a senior, right? Is everyone driving you nuts, asking you about your life's ambitions?"

"You remember how that was, huh?"

"Crikey, do I ever. It was like, please, just ask me how my day was or tell me you hate my hair or something. *Anything* except The Question."

"I don't hate your hair."

She laughed, and her eyes sparkled a bit. Green—they kind of matched her hair. And they made me think of Nat. I'm a sucker for green eyes.

"Well, whatever my life's ambitions are," I said, "I'm gonna be flipping burgers for a while so I can pay you guys off."

She looked thoughtful. "You know, we're hiring a new trainee. Bob usually goes for people from the technical college, but if you're looking, maybe you should talk to him. He could teach you a lot about analyzing photos from the forensics side."

"Wow," I said. "Cool. Yeah, thanks. I'll definitely give him a call." Suddenly I remembered that I was grounded. I was supposed to have gone straight home from the meeting at school. Whoops.

I told Charlotte good night, hustled home, and rushed inside with a carefully prepared excuse on the tip of my tongue.

My mom swooped in on me and folded me into a giant hug.

"Oh, Kaito," she said. "Your principal called. Your father and I are so—"

"Mom," I said. "Mom, it's okay. Just let go of me before I smother." She giggled and released me.

"Kaito," my dad said, "Principal Juarez assured us that this—this so-called suspension has been taken off your record. And your teachers will allow you to make up the work you missed."

It's funny what a single day can do. Yesterday, my parents could barely stand the sight of me. Today, it's all smiles and hugs and "let's go out to dinner." Which we did, to my favorite steak joint.

First, though, we caught the local news. Sure enough, the reporter who had come to my school updated the story:

"The Woodrow Wilson High School teacher accused of cheating on standardized tests has resigned. Michelle Opal, math instructor and cheerleading coach for eight years, has declined to comment. But school officials confirmed today that a student's photographs showing the alleged cheating have been authenticated by an expert."

The camera cut to Principal Juarez. "This very unfortunate incident illustrates what can happen when teachers lose sight of what's most important in the classroom: teaching."

My dad made an approving noise and turned off the TV. "My son, the investigative reporter," he said with a grin. "Who knows, Kaito, maybe you have a future in journalism!"

"Actually," I said as we piled into the car to go to dinner, "I might be getting a job at the digital forensics firm that validated my photos. I owe them a lot of money."

"Hmm," Mom said. "I'm sure your father and I can help out with that. It isn't right that you've had to deal with this all on your own. But if you're interested in—what did you say it's called?"

"Digital forensics."

"Digital forensics, then that's great too."

As I munched on my steak a few minutes later, I wondered what I'd have been eating for dinner tonight if I hadn't proven my case. Microwaved hot dogs, probably.

It was good to be in the clear. That was for sure.

CHAPTER SIXTEEN

On my way to school the next morning, I stopped by an ATM and drained the rest of my bank account. That left me with nothing to pay Mr. McNamara, but at least I'd have some help from my parents there.

First, though, I had to deal with my classes. We had a substitute in trig. She looked flustered even before the bell rang, like she knew she was in for a rough day.

"Ms. Opal will not be teaching for, uh, the rest of the semester, due to some . . . personal issues," the sub explained over a sea of whispers. "I'm Ms. Barnum. I'll be with you until the school finds a long-term replacement."

Vince shot up his hand and started talking before the sub called on him. "Did Ms. Opal get fired?"

Ms. Barnum sighed. "I'm not at liberty to discuss the details," she said. "Let's all open our textbooks to page 118. We have a lot to cover . . . "

Vince high-fived me across the aisle. Ms. Barnum pretended not to notice.

Things just got better from there. People started congratulating me in the hallways as word spread that I'd been telling the truth all along.

"I knew you had it right, man," said some guy I didn't even know.

"Dude, way to show that cheater what's up!" said another.

Even Kevin Scofield had a decent word for me. Sort of. "Nicely done, Sushi!" he proclaimed, to the usual snickers from his crew.

And then, waiting at my locker after US history, there was Nat.

She looked like maybe she hadn't been sleeping too well. And she didn't smile when she saw me, just put up her hand and gave a sort of a half wave.

"Hey," I said.

"Hey."

I didn't really know what to say next. I mean, she was the one who'd had the last word, and it hadn't been a friendly one. So I just waited.

"Kai," she said, "I should have believed you. I'm sorry." She looked so sad, like she'd lost something really important to her. Which I guess she had.

"Yeah," I said. "I wish you'd trusted me. But I get it."

"You do?"

And in that moment, I did. "Ms. Opal was your coach for what, three years? And all your friends were telling you I had to have lied."

She nodded. "Yeah," she said softly.

For a minute, I started remembering what it felt like to hold her.

"I still think what you did was wrong, though."

"Huh?"

"You didn't have to expose her like that to everyone," Nat said. "You probably ruined her whole life."

"I just told the truth—"

"Yeah, yeah, the truth," Nat said. "I know. But is this what she really deserved? How's she ever going to get another teaching job?"

I didn't have an answer to that. To be honest, I really hadn't thought about what would happen to Ms. Opal. I'd wanted to show her up as the cheater she was, and then I'd wanted to clear my name. Maybe Nat was right—maybe I'd gone too far.

"I did what I thought was right," I said finally. "And I can't take it back now."

"No," she said. "You can't." She met my gaze one more time. "See you around, Kai."

And then she was gone.

CHAPTER SEVENTEEN

By the end of the day, I was exhausted. I felt like I'd told my story a million times. People couldn't get enough of it, especially the part about Juarez apologizing to me. Not really his style, you know? So it was major news.

When the final bell rang, I set out to deal with the last loose end.

I knew where to find him—after all, I'd studied his patterns back before all this started, back when I was planning to break into Ms. Opal's desk. After the last bell, he takes care of the cafeteria.

Sure enough, there he was.

"Hey, Sully," I said.

"Photographer Kai," he replied, setting down his mop. "Right on schedule."

Hardly anybody was around, just a couple people at the vending machines. But I wasn't about to take any chances, not this late in the game.

"Just wanted to thank you again for helping me out," I said, offering my hand.

Sully gave me a firm shake, and I slipped him the cash. My last hundred bucks, well spent.

Sure, I probably would've gotten the suspension lifted even without a witness from Juarez's own staff, but with him? It was a slam dunk. I wondered what Ms. Opal thought about my methods. Not for the first time, I realized that they weren't all that different from her own. She was just the one who got caught.

Now it was all over. I'd done what I had to do. But I couldn't quite make myself forget that Ms. Opal had actually been a great teacher. The kind who made stuff interesting—the kind who thought her students were interesting. The kind that people like Nat would shed tears over.

Yeah, I thought I needed to cheat on her trig exam, but it wasn't her fault that I sucked at math. I probably would've done better if I'd studied more instead of spending all that time planning to steal the answer key. And Nat had made a good point. Opal would probably never teach again, at least not around here.

On TV, Juarez had said that Ms. Opal lost sight of the importance of teaching. But what she did had nothing to do with teaching. A lot of people think those ARA tests are completely bogus. Cheating on them didn't mean Ms. Opal didn't care about helping us learn.

At the end of the day, she had cheated and lied. And so had I. That was something I was going to have to learn to live with.

● ● ●

On my way home, I swung into the park and went to look at the creek. I hadn't been here for a week. In fact, I hadn't used my camera at all since the Opal photos. I pulled it out of my backpack and held it for a minute, thinking about how much had changed in that short time.

The late afternoon light played out over the water in a new way. The shadows seemed longer somehow. Not completely dark but darker than before. I adjusted the camera's settings, held it up, and clicked away. It took a few tries, but this time I managed a perfect shot.

ABOUT THE AUTHOR

Shannon Knudsen has written many books for young readers. She lives with her cat and her dog in Arizona.

THE ALTERNATIVE

FAILING CLASSES.

DROPPING OUT.

JAIL TIME.

When it seems like there are no other options left, Rondo Alternative High School might just be the last chance a student needs.

THE ALTERNATIVE

BARRIER
PATRICK JONES

THE ALTERNATIVE

BRIDGE
PATRICK JONES

THE ALTERNATIVE

CONTROLLED
PATRICK JONES

THE ALTERNATIVE

OUTBURST
PATRICK JONES

THE ALTERNATIVE

TARGET
PATRICK JONES

WINNING IS *NOT OPTIONAL.*